The THREE DOTS

Elise Primavera

G. P. PUTNAM'S SONS
NEW YORK

Library of Congress Cataloging-in-
Publication Data. Primavera, Elise.
The Three Dots / Elise Primavera.
p. cm.   Summary: Three dotted
animals, a frog, duck, and moose, enjoy
playing together and form a band, but
their friendship is endangered
as the fortunes of their band rise
and continue to change. [1. Bands
(Music)—Fiction. 2. Friendship—
Fiction. 3. Frogs—Fiction.
4. Ducks—Fiction. 5. Moose—
Fiction.] I. Title.   PZ7.P9354Th
1993. [E]—dc20 92-12979 CIP AC
ISBN 0-399-22429-7
10 9 8 7 6 5 4 3 2 1   First Impression

Henry was from South Jersey, Sal was born in Alaska and Margaret came from the Midwest. Although they lived in different parts of the country, they did have a few things in common. The most obvious of which were DOTS.

Their lives were difficult.

To feel less lonely, Henry, Margaret and Sal
turned to music.

When they were old enough they left home
to seek their fortunes in New York City.

And by some strange twist of fate, they all walked into the same donut shop.

Things we have in common:
1. DOTS
2. MUSIC
3. No where to live.

BIG DONUTS

It wasn't long before they knew they were kindred spirits.

They decided to get an apartment together.

Every night Henry, Sal and Margaret watched TV and ate donuts.

Every day they played together. For the first time
in their lives they were happy.

One day they answered an ad in the paper.

"What do you kids call yourselves?" Honey Goldstar
asked. Without thinking, Sal answered, "THE THREE DOTS!"

"I like it, I like it," Honey said, and signed them up
on the spot.

The Three Dots started out playing in little downtown clubs.

Their popularity grew. They made appearances on all the talk shows. They were interviewed and photographed. People sought their advice on everything.

They played for
the president.

They played for
the Queen of England.

They played for
MADONNA!

Then something curious started to happen.
On talk shows, for instance, the host would address
Sal and not Henry or Margaret. People would ask Sal
for his autograph and ignore Henry and Margaret.

Offers started to pour in. The final straw came when Hollywood proposed a deal for a movie called *Sal's Hawaiian Luau.*

Sal's part was to sing to hundreds of adoring islanders and tourists. Henry had a part as an islander. Margaret had a part as a tourist.

Henry moved into his own apartment. He decided to fulfill a lifelong ambition and took up painting.

Margaret bought a Big O Donut Shop.
"I'll keep in touch," Henry said.
"We'll have lunch," Margaret said.

But they never did.
Their birthdays passed and so did Christmas.

Then it was a year to the day since
Henry, Sal and Margaret met.

Henry decided to send a message to Margaret.

At the same time Margaret was making
a message for Henry.

Sal sent a message to both of them.

By some strange twist of fate, all their messages
were exactly the same.

And from that day on, Henry, Sal and Margaret
got along famously.